D0999594

PAMPALCHE OF THE SILVER TEETH

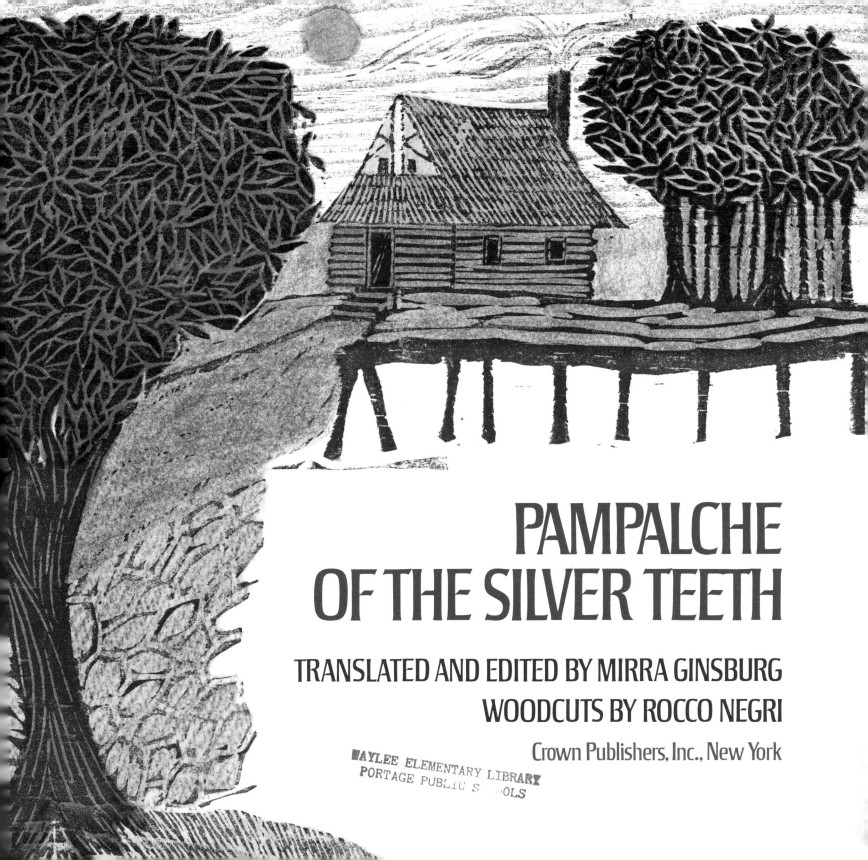

PAMPALCHE
OF THE SILVER TEETH

TRANSLATED AND EDITED BY MIRRA GINSBURG
WOODCUTS BY ROCCO NEGRI

Crown Publishers, Inc., New York

Library of Congress Cataloging in Publication Data

Ginsburg, Mirra.
    Pampalche of the silver teeth.

    SUMMARY: A beautiful girl, in an effort to escape marriage to the
Master of the Waters, journeys through the forest towards safety,
only to be pursued by an evil witch.

    [1. Folklore — Russia]   I. Negri, Rocco.
II. Title.
PZ8.1.G455Pam   398.2'2'0947   [E]   75-6794
ISBN 0-517-52241-1

A long time ago, in the woods where the Mari people lived, there was an old hunter. His wife was dead, his older daughter had gone to live elsewhere, and the only joy of his life was his younger daughter, lovely as the moon, with teeth as white as silver. The people sang songs about her and called her Pampalche of the Silver Teeth. The old man hunted in the woods and fished in the lake; his daughter gathered berries in the forest, and that was how they lived. And though she was alone all day, Pampalche was never lonely, for all the beasts and birds in the woods were her friends.

One morning her father went to the lake to fish, and Pampalche went to the woods for berries.

She found a sunny clearing where the ground was covered with ripe red strawberries and began to pick them. She plucked berry after berry, eating some, and putting the others into her little basket. And she sang:

> "Where the bright sun rises
> the sky glows like a bonfire.
> The dawn glows like a bonfire,
> the bright sun rises
> And warms the night-chilled earth."

Pampalche raised her head and looked around her. She saw a gray cuckoo on a tree and smiled a welcome to it. Then she sang again:

> "My father is fishing in the lake,
>   and I am gathering strawberries.
>   In the clearing,
>   among white blossoms,
>   I gather berries every day."

When her basket was filled to the rim with ripe berries, Pampalche turned homeward.

She walked along the forest path till she came to a dark green fir tree. On the fir tree sat a black raven. He flapped his huge black wings and nodded at the girl. Pampalche stopped and asked in a frightened voice:

"Why do you nod at me, black raven? Why do you flap your wings? Does any misfortune lie in wait for me?"

The raven did not answer.

Pampalche did not know that at this very moment her father suddenly was overcome with thirst. He bent down to the water and touched his lips to it. Black, crested waves rose on the lake, the water raged and foamed and swirled, and a huge dark hand stretched out from the depths. It seized the old man's beard and started pulling him into the lake. The fisherman was filled with terror and begged the Master of the Waters:

"O great, dread Master of the Waters! Do not destroy me, let me go!"

And the Master of the Waters answered:

"I will let you go and will permit you to fish in all my lakes and rivers if you give me your daughter Pampalche of the Silver Teeth to be my wife."

The old man wept and pleaded, but the Master of the Waters would not relent.

"I have no choice," thought the father. "If I die, Pampalche will perish by herself."

And he agreed to let the Master of the Waters marry Pampalche.

"Come to my house tomorrow," he said. "Bring twelve buckets of mead and twelve buckets of ale, and we shall celebrate the wedding."

The huge dark hand released the old man's beard.

"But mind you, don't forget your promise!" the Master said. "Wait for me tomorrow."

The old man walked sadly homeward. He walked, and tripped on roots and stumps, his mind filled with bitter thoughts.

At home Pampalche asked him:

"What makes you so sad, Father?"

The old man sighed and answered:

"The steps to our hut are cracked and broken. I have nothing to fix them with."

"Don't worry, Father, I have the boards all ready. Tomorrow we shall fix the steps."

But the father looked even sadder than before. And his daughter asked again:

"What else makes you so sad, Father?"

"Our roof has rotted from last autumn's rains. It leaks."

"That is no trouble, either," said Pampalche. "We shall cover it tomorrow with fresh straw."

And now the old man hung his head and said:

"It's neither steps nor roof that trouble me. I promised you, dear daughter, as wife to the Master of the Waters. Tomorrow he will come to marry you and take you to his underwater kingdom."

The old man wept bitterly, but his daughter consoled him:

"Stop grieving, Father! I will escape from the Master of the Waters. I will go to my sister, beyond the distant woods, on the high mountain. He will never reach me there."

And Pampalche put on her oldest, shabbiest dress, pasted thick pine resin over her silver teeth, and bid her father a warm farewell.

"My daughter," the old man said to her in parting. "May every trouble miss you on the way! May you meet no enemies! May neither the Master of the Waters nor his servants lay their hands on you!"

Pampalche bowed low to her father, embraced him, and set out on her distant journey—beyond the dense woods, to the mountain where her sister lived.

She walked through deep, dark forests, over dismal bogs. In the daytime she begged the sun to show her the way; at night she begged the moon to lead her. The bright sun showed her the way in daytime, the white moon lit her path at night.

On the second day Pampalche heard the sound of horns and caught sight of the Master of the Waters in the distance. He rode a stallion black as a black raven. On either side of him walked youths in snow-white caftans, carrying green birch twigs. "Too-oo, too-oo!" The Master of the Waters blew loudly into his golden horn, so loudly that the trees shook and the birds grew silent.

Pampalche dug herself into the soft moss by the wayside, and the Master of the Waters rode by without seeing her. When he was far away, she came out of her hiding place and continued her journey.

She met young girls in green wedding cloaks and shawls embroidered with bright, gleaming spangles.

"Where are you going, sisters?" Pampalche asked.

And the girls answered with a song:

> *"We are going for the bride,*
> *for the beautiful bride with the silver teeth*
> *and a face as lovely as the moon.*
> *We are bringing twelve buckets of mead*
> *and twelve buckets of ale.*
> *We are going for Pampalche of the Silver Teeth,*
> *to take her to the Master of the Waters."*

"Go, hurry," Pampalche said. "She has been waiting for you for a long time."

And she went on.

She met old men in festive clothes.
"Where are you going, uncles?" Pampalche asked.
And the old men answered with a song:

> "We are going for the bride,
> Pampalche of the Silver Teeth,
> lovely as the moon,
> bright as a star.
> We are bringing twelve buckets of honey
> and twelve buckets of butter."

"Go on, go on," said Pampalche. "Hurry. The bride can
barely wait to see you."
And she went on.

She met old women in bright kerchiefs.

"Where are you going, aunties?" Pampalche asked.

And the old women answered with a song:

> *"We are going for the bride,*
> *Pampalche of the Silver Teeth,*
> *bright as the moon,*
> *lovely as the sun.*
> *We are bringing twelve buckets of milk*
> *and twelve buckets of cheese."*

"Hurry, hurry," said Pampalche. "She cannot wait to see you."

And she went on.

She walked through the forest and saw an old woman limping toward her, so old that she was moss-grown all over like an ancient tree stump.

"Where are you going, grandma?" Pampalche asked.

The old crone mumbled something toothlessly and sang in a hoarse voice:

> *"I am going for the bride,*
>   *the beautiful bride with the silver teeth,*
>   *her cheeks as rosy as ripe strawberries,*
>   *her face as lovely as the sun."*

Pampalche laughed, and the pine resin dropped from her teeth. The crone looked at her and gloated.

"Ah-h! You are Pampalche of the Silver Teeth!" she cried and clutched her with her bony fingers. "You won't escape me. I will take you to the Master of the Waters!"

Pampalche broke away from the old crone and ran. She ran, she flew as swiftly as a bird, but the crone kept up with her: she ran as swiftly as the girl, because she was not simply an old woman, but the terrible witch Voover-Coove herself.

Pampalche ran across a wide field, through a great dark forest, and at last she reached the mountain where her sister lived. But now she was so tired that she could barely take another step. She could not scale the mountain, and Voover-Coove was not far behind her. Another moment, and she'd have her in her clutches once again.

Pampalche climbed up a tall pine tree and sang:

> *"Oh, sister, sister,*
> *let down a silken ladder!*
> *Or Voover-Coove will catch me*
> *and take me to the Master of the Waters."*

Voover-Coove ran up to the pine, broke off one of her bony fingers, pulled out one of her crooked teeth, and made herself an axe. Then she began to chop down the pine tree where Pampalche sat.

"Oh, sister, sister!" cried Pampalche.

And her sister answered from the mountain:

"Wait, dear Pampalche, till I unwind the ball of silken thread."

A brown bear came out of the woods and lumbered up to Voover-Coove.

"You must be weary, grandma," he said. "I'll chop the pine for you. Lie down and take a rest."

So Voover-Coove gave the bear her axe, lay down under a bush, and fell asleep.

The bear lifted the axe and threw it into the nearby lake.

Voover-Coove woke up: no bear, no axe, nothing but circles spreading on the surface of the lake. The old crone flew into a rage, sucked up the water from the lake in a single breath, picked up her axe from the bottom, and began to chop again.

A loud noise spread through the woods, the tall pine shook, and Pampalche sang still more loudly:

> "Oh, sister, sister,
> let down the silken ladder!
> Or Voover-Coove will catch me
> and take me to the Master of the Waters."

And the sister answered her again from the top of the high mountain:

"Wait, dear Pampalche, till I plait the silken ladder."

The red fox heard Pampalche's song. She came running to the pine and said to Voover-Coove:

"Oh, what a tall, thick pine! You must be weary, grandma. Give me the axe, I'll help you!"

Voover-Coove believed the red fox and gave her the axe. And that was all the red fox needed. She struck one blow at the pine, raised the axe, and threw it far into the lake.

Once more Voover-Coove drank up all the water in the lake, snatched the axe from the bottom, and began to chop the pine.

Pampalche sang her song again:

"*Oh, sister, sister,*
   let down the silken ladder!
   Voover-Coove is about to catch me
   and give me to the Master of the Waters."

Her sister did not answer.

The pine tree creaked, bent, and began to fall. But at this moment the silken ladder came down from above. Pampalche of the Silver Teeth caught it and quickly climbed up the high mountain to join her sister.

The evil Voover-Coove gnashed her teeth and howled with rage. She could not get Pampalche anymore, because the magic of a silken ladder destroys the magic of a witch.

And when the forest beasts saw that their friend Pampalche of the Silver Teeth was safe, they laughed and danced with joy. The birds in the green branches burst into loud song, and Pampalche answered merrily from the high mountain:

> "I've had the sun to light my day,
> I've had the moon to point my way.
> Along the shiny silken ladder
> I climbed up the high mountain.
> Voover-Coove will not catch me now,
> she will not give me
> to the Master of the Waters.
> I will not have to spend my life
> as the hateful monster's wife."

MIRRA GINSBURG is a distinguished translator of Russian literature. *The Diary of Nina Kosterina*, *The Kaha Bird*, and *The White Ship* were nominees for the Mildred L. Batchelder Award. Her most recent book for Crown, *How Wilka Went to Sea and Other Tales from West of the Urals*, illustrated by Charles Mikolaycak, received excellent reviews everywhere, including starred reviews in *School Library Journal* and *Booklist*. Ms. Ginsburg makes her home in New York City.

ROCCO NEGRI spent his childhood in Buenos Aires, Argentina, and now lives with his wife and two children in Ridgewood, New York. He received his art training at the Art Students League of New York and the School of Visual Arts. Of his woodcuts for *The Son of the Leopard* by Harold Courlander (a 1974 ALA Notable Children's Book), *Publishers Weekly* said, "Negri's woodcuts are brilliant accompaniments to a compelling legend."